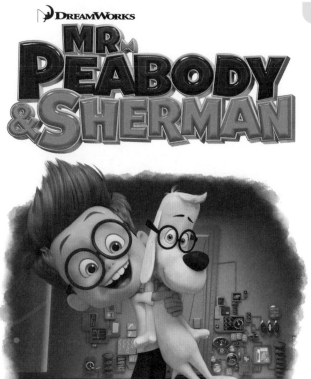

FRIENDS from WAY BACK!

By Billy Wrecks

A Random House PICTUREBACK® Book

Random House 🏠 New York

randomhouse.com/kids
ISBN 978-0-385-37528-3
MANUFACTURED IN CHINA
10 9 8 7 6 5 4 3 2

MR. PEABODY

is a genius, an inventor, and, most importantly, the father of a boy named Sherman. And even though Mr. Peabody is a dog, they love each other like any father and son do.

Mr. Peabody created a time machine called the WABAC (pronounced "way back") to teach Sherman all about important events in history. Sometimes they end up in some very strange situations when they go on their adventures! But they also meet important people and make interesting friends. . . .

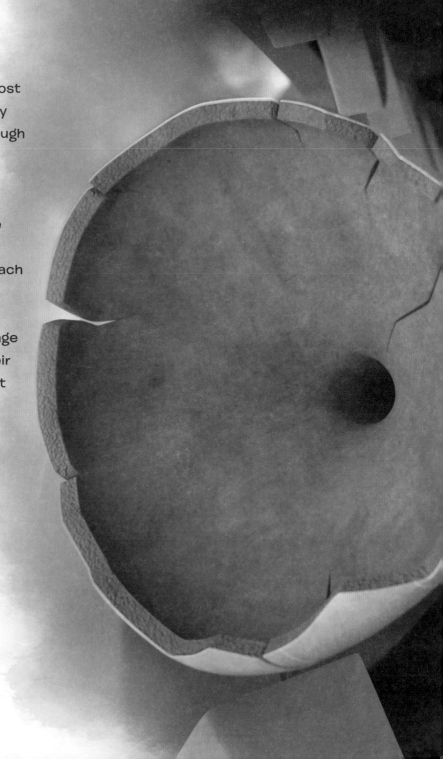

KING TUT, THE BOY PHARAOH

Once, when Sherman took his friend Penny on a trip in the WABAC, she ended up engaged to marry **King Tut**, the boy ruler of ancient Egypt.

Luckily, Mr. Peabody and Sherman were able to rescue her. They barely escaped after the heartbroken king sent his guards to capture them!

ROBESPIERRE AND THE FRENCH REVOLUTION

While visiting the Queen of France during the time of the French Revolution, Mr. Peabody and Sherman came face to face with **Robespierre**.

He was the leader of the French revolutionaries who wanted to get rid of the monarchy—and Mr. Peabody.

Mr. Peabody's quick swordplay and quick thinking allowed him and Sherman to make a quick getaway!

LEONARDO DA VINCI, RENAISSANCE MAN

The famous painter of the *Mona Lisa*, **Leonardo da Vinci**, was an old friend of Mr. Peabody's. Also an inventor, Leonardo helped Mr. Peabody recharge the WABAC after it made an emergency landing during the Renaissance, over 500 years ago.

Leonardo was surprised when Sherman and Penny took his flying machine for a ride. He didn't know that it actually worked!

AGAMEMNON AND THE TROJAN HORSE

During another trip to the past, Sherman decided to join the Greek army just as they were about to sneak into the walled city of Troy using a giant wooden horse. The Greek general **Agamemnon** took a real liking to Sherman and gave him armor, a sword, and a Greek name: **Shermanus!**

Mr. Peabody had to rescue Sherman—and once again,
they barely escaped with their lives!

SHOCKED SHERMAN

Time travel is a tricky business, and the strangest person Sherman met turned out to be . . .

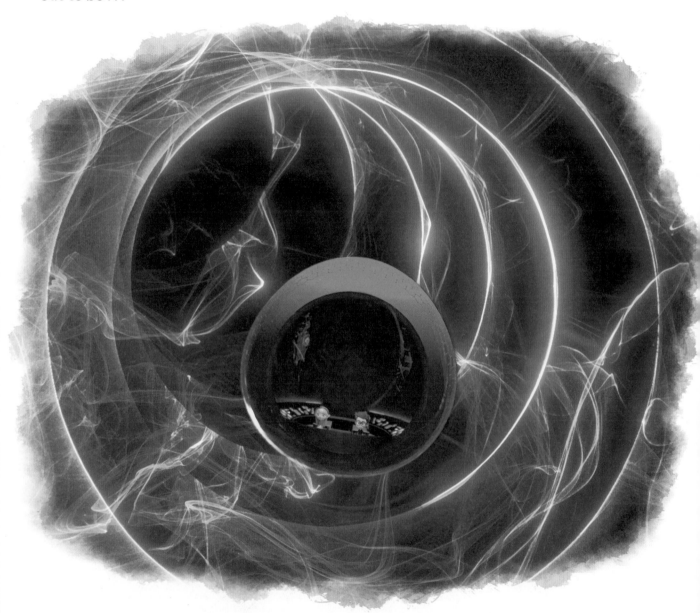

...ANOTHER SHERMAN!

Sherman traveled back to the
present to get help from Mr. Peabody,
but he showed up too soon and met
himself from another time! When
the two boys touched, they started
to morph back together, and then
the whole space-time continuum
went **KA-BLOOEY!** People from
throughout the past started showing
up in the present.

Luckily, **Mr. Peabody** and **Sherman** were able to fix the universe and send all their friends back to where they belonged in the past. And even though they didn't know where their adventures would take them next, the future looked bright for this amazing father and son.

© DreamWorks Animation L.L.C.

TO THE WABAC!

PEABODY KNOWS BEST

Trust me, I'VE BEEN THERE

KABLOOEY!

But Mr. Peabody told Sherman to come down immediately. And that's just what Sherman did—**CRASH!** Thankfully, nobody was hurt, and Sherman and Penny had had a great time.

The WABAC was recharged and ready to take them home. And even though Mr. Peabody was a little bit mad at him, Sherman was exhilarated because he had mastered the art of flying!

When Mr. Peabody and Leonardo saw them, Leonardo yelled, **"My flying machine—it works! And, Sherman, you are the first flying boy!"**

Penny made Sherman take the controls. To Sherman's surprise, he turned out to be great at flying.

"This is crazy," Sherman protested.

Sherman was happy to show Penny the machine's mechanisms. But before he knew what was happening, she had pulled a lever, which launched the flying machine into the air. Sherman and Penny went soaring over the town!

"Just tell me how it works," Penny said innocently.

Penny climbed into the cockpit of Leonardo's flying machine. She wanted to take it for a ride, but Sherman didn't think that was such a good idea. **"We should probably just leave that alone,"** he warned.

Sherman and Penny found Leonardo's attic, which was full of his inventions.
"It's like a toy store!" Penny said with delight.

Since Leonardo and Mr. Peabody were busy, Sherman and Penny went to explore.

Leonardo and Mr. Peabody set to work building a contraption to recharge the WABAC.

Sherman tried to assist Mr. Peabody, but he kept getting in the way. When he tried to help Leonardo, the famous inventor quickly said, **"Ahhh! No! No! That's quite all right."**

Luckily, Mr. Peabody was good friends with the artist Leonardo da Vinci, someone he knew could help. Leonardo was famous for painting the *Mona Lisa*. But like Mr. Peabody, Leonardo was also an inventor.

"We're in a desperate hurry to get home, but the WABAC needs a jump start," Mr. Peabody said. "We thought, 'Who better than Leonardo da Vinci to help us on our way?'"

Leonardo gladly agreed to help.

Now Mr. Peabody, Sherman, and Penny were hurtling through time and looking for a place to land. The WABAC was almost out of fuel. Working the controls, Mr. Peabody aimed the time machine toward Renaissance Italy, around 500 years in the past.

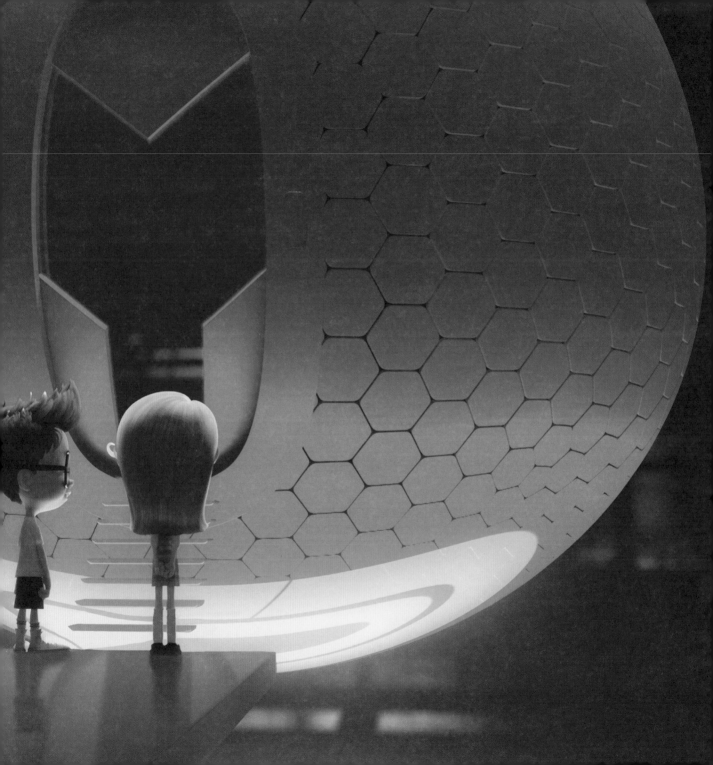

Sherman was a boy like most boys his age. But his father, Mr. Peabody, was an extraordinary genius, a scientist, an inventor . . . and a dog. Together they had made many trips into the past using Mr. Peabody's time machine, called the **WABAC** (pronounced "way back"), to learn about great moments in history.

Their latest adventure started when Sherman showed his friend Penny the WABAC. They took it for a ride, which was something Mr. Peabody had told Sherman **not** to do!

THE ART OF FLYING!

By Billy Wrecks

A Random House PICTUREBACK® Book

Random House 🏠 New York

"Mr. Peabody & Sherman" © 2014 DreamWorks Animation L.L.C. Character rights TM & © Ward Productions, Inc. Licensed by Bullwinkle Studios, LLC. All rights reserved. Published in the United States by Random House Children's Books, a division of Random House LLC, 1745 Broadway, New York, NY 10019, and in Canada by Random House of Canada Limited, Toronto, Penguin Random House Companies. Pictureback, Random House, and the Random House colophon are registered trademarks of Random House LLC.
randomhouse.com/kids
ISBN 978-0-385-37528-3
MANUFACTURED IN CHINA
10 9 8 7 6 5 4 3 2